Lincoln School Library

DRUG DANGERS

ALCOHOL DRUG DANGERS

Lawrence Clayton, Ph.D.

Enslow Publishers, Inc.

44 Fadem Road   PO Box 38
Box 699   Aldershot
Springfield, NJ 07081   Hants GU12 6BP
USA   UK

http://www.enslow.com

To: The Reverend Nick Harris

Library of Congress Cataloging-in-Publication Data

Clayton, L. (Lawrence)
    Alcohol drug dangers / Lawrence Clayton.
        p. cm. — (Drug dangers)
    Includes bibliographical references (p.) and index.
    Summary: Examines the popularity and social impact of alcohol, discusses the dangers of alcohol abuse, and offers suggestions on how to get help for those with a drinking problem.
    ISBN 0-7660-1159-3 -
    1. Alcoholism—Juvenile literature. 2. Teenagers—Alcohol use—Juvenile literature. [1. Alcoholism.] I. Title II. Series
HV5066.C53   1999
362.292—dc21   98-35776
                                                          CIP
                                                          AC

Printed in the United States of America

10 9 8 7 6 5 4 3 2 1

To our Readers:
All Internet addresses in this book were active and appropriate when we went to press. Any comments or suggestions can be sent by e-mail to Comments@enslow.com or to the address on the back cover.

Photo Credits: Corel Corporation, pp. 6, 7, 11, 12, 14, 20, 27, 30, 33, 35, 44 (bottom left); Díamar Interactive Corp., pp. 39, 44 (top right), 45, 48; New England Stock Photos, © Clifford Keeney, p. 18; New England Stock Photos, © John and Diane Harper, pp. 17, 24.

Cover Photo: Corel Corporation

contents

Titles in the **Drug Dangers** series:

Alcohol Drug Dangers
ISBN 0-7660-1159-3

Crack and Cocaine Drug Dangers
ISBN 0-7660-1155-0

Diet Pill Drug Dangers
ISBN 0-7660-1158-5

Heroin Drug Dangers
ISBN 0-7660-1156-9

Inhalant Drug Dangers
ISBN 0-7660-1153-4

Marijuana Drug Dangers
ISBN 0-7660-1214-X

Speed and Methamphetamine Drug Dangers
ISBN 0-7660-1157-7

Steroid Drug Dangers
ISBN 0-7660-1154-2

A Popular Poison

"Jon" (not his real name) was just five years old when he took his first drink, and he hated it.[1] He remembered his father and his friends laughing at him as his throat burned, causing tears to fill his eyes. His father said, "It ain't Sprite™, is it son?"

Jon never touched alcohol again until he was eleven. He was at a crawfish boil—a huge party where his family and their friends feasted on crawfish (a type of spiny lobster), red beans, and rice. And there was lots of beer. After that, he drank every chance he got.

When he was fourteen, he got his driver's license. (Jon lived in Louisiana, one of the few states that licenses drivers that young.) This made buying beer easy, because New Orleans was filled with stores that sold beer to minors. One store manager, who typically sold to minors, used to ask for his driver's license so the security cameras

Unfortunately, as was the case for Jon in Louisiana, in some states it is all too easy for underage drinkers to buy alcohol.

would have a tape of Jon showing it to him if there was a problem. Then he would sell Jon and his friends all the beer they wanted. By summer, Jon was drinking a twelve-pack five to six nights a week.

On his fifteenth birthday, his friends introduced him to wine coolers. He downed eight that night. He and his friends partied almost every night. Soon he was drinking twelve to eighteen wine coolers an evening.

Jon cannot remember when he started using hard liquor. But he does remember being in a park with a friend the summer he turned sixteen. They had a quart of vodka, which they chugged straight down in about thirty minutes. Jon was so drunk that he ran as hard as he could, head first, into a tree. Passersby found him sitting on the ground with tree bark sticking out of his head and blood running down his face. They recognized him and called his parents. When they arrived, he started a fistfight with his father, who finally knocked Jon out and took him home. When he awoke the next morning, he was laying in his vomit-soaked clothes and his mother was wiping his face with a washcloth.

Jon dropped out of school when he was seventeen. Soon after that, he started drinking again. By the time he was twenty-one, he was hanging out at New Orleans bars. He remembered standing in a bar and shaking so badly he could not get a drink to his mouth without spilling it. Someone came over, grabbed the bottle, and

Although Jon needed alcohol to stop his body from shaking, and he knew this was a sure sign of trouble, he was still unable to stop drinking.

stuck it into his mouth. Jon drank eagerly and long. In a few minutes, the shaking stopped. He knew then that he was in trouble, but he still could not quit.

A year later, he was at a club and very drunk. Someone sprayed an inhalant on his shirtsleeve and he sniffed it. Then everything went black. All he remembered was being in an ambulance and someone shouting, "Don't die on me!" over and over. After he got out of the hospital, Jon remembered, he liked being alone in dark places. He would just find a place—under some steps, in an alley, in the garage—and drink.

Then one of his friends went for treatment and got sober. He began encouraging Jon to do the same. At first, Jon just laughed at him. But one morning when Jon was really sick, his friend came by. He took one look at Jon and said, "You never have to feel this way again if you don't want to." At the time, all Jon could think about was getting a drink, but later he kept thinking about what his

Alcohol Use and Abuse in the United States

90 percent of high school seniors use alcohol.[2]

30 percent of high school seniors abuse alcohol.[3]

Some one hundred thousand ten-and eleven-year-olds get drunk every week.[4]

Of the estimated 11 million alcoholics in the United States, 3 million are teenagers.[5]

friend had said. A week later, he went for treatment. That was two years ago.

Jon finished high school and started college. He also got married. But he still fears alcohol's powerful hold. "Some days," he says, "it's all I can do to resist alcohol. I pray to God that I'll make it!"

two

The Social Impact of Alcohol

Alcohol is at the root of many of the social problems that Americans face today. Let's take a closer look at a some of them.

Drunk Driving

Drunk driving is a serious problem in our society. In fact, drunk driving is the most common crime committed in the United States.[1] In 1994, about five hundred sixty thousand people were injured by drunk drivers. They were the lucky ones. Almost eighteen thousand were killed, and twenty-nine hundred of them were children and youth. That's about eight young people who die as a result of drunk driving every day.[2]

Although such statistics are impersonal, the tragedies behind them are painfully real. Our society is losing some of its finest people. One example is the death of Princess Diana. The driver of the car, Henri Paul, was allegedly drunk. His blood alcohol level was three times the legal limit under French law. Dr. Jack Cornelius, professor of psychiatry at the University of Pittsburgh, claimed that was more than enough to have played a part in the accident.[3]

The driver got off work at 7:00 P.M. and went to a popular bar near the hotel in Paris, France, where the princess and her boyfriend, Dodi Al Fayed, were having dinner. About 10:00 P.M., he was called on a cellular phone to come back to work. He did so, but never bothered to inform anyone that he had been drinking heavily. At 12:21 A.M. he drove away with Mr. Al Fayed, the princess, and her bodyguard. He entered a tunnel, where the speed limit was 45 miles per hour, doing somewhere between 80 and 121 miles per hour.

Drinking and driving are a deadly combination. Decision making and reflexes are compromised when alcohol is consumed, and the results can be tragic.

Princess Diana's tragic death in an automobile accident in Paris, France, was a devastating loss to society.

Swerving to pass a slower moving car, he lost control and slammed into a cement pillar. The driver and Dodi Al Fayed died immediately. It took rescuers over an hour to cut the princess out of the car. She died a few hours later at a hospital. The only survivor was her bodyguard, and he was seriously injured. He returned to France following the accident to testify about what he remembered.[4]

Another example of the tragedies connected with drunk driving was the Matli family of Piedmont, Oklahoma. The Matli children, Trevor (twelve), Marcus (fifteen), and Jennifer (seventeen) went to school with the children of this book's author. Mark Matli was a veterinarian. His wife, Marilyn, helped him with his practice. On January 3, 1995, they were just sitting down to dinner when a neighbor called to say he had hit a bobcat on the way home. He wondered if Mr. Matli would come to help the animal.

The whole family went to the scene in the family van. They found the injured bobcat at the bottom of a small hill. Mr. Matli worked on the animal as the rest of the family watched and helped as best they could. Jennifer was cold, so she got back into the van to get warm. A moment later, a pickup truck came speeding over the top of the hill. Mark yelled to his family to run for the ditch beside the road. They got there just as the driver of the pickup realized that there were vehicles ahead. He swerved into the ditch to avoid them. Trevor, Marcus, and their mother were killed instantly. Jennifer was able to spend a few minutes with her father before he lost consciousness. He spent that time encouraging her to go on with her life. He died at Mercy Hospital at 6:00 A.M. the next morning. The driver of the pickup truck was a teenager, and he was drunk.[5]

Football should be a fun, recreational activity for young people to play and watch. However, both college and professional teams have shown that alcohol and football do not mix.

Not everyone who drives drunk causes a tragedy, but the potential for tragedy always exists. Let's look at what happened to the University of Nebraska's football team in 1996. The team lost three of its starting players because of suspensions for drunk driving. First, their defensive captain was kicked off the team after his second drunk driving arrest. Then, a senior wingback was suspended. The second-string wingback had been arrested for driving under the influence (DUI) of alcohol a few months earlier.[6]

It is not just college teams, but also the National Football League (NFL) that has these problems. The Carolina Panthers ran into trouble in 1994. The team's center was suspended for an alcohol-related car crash.

As a result, he spent twenty-six days at the Betty Ford Center.[7]

Crime and Violence

Although it is true that drunk driving is a crime, it is certainly not the only crime associated with drinking. In fact, crime and violence are often a part of alcohol abuse.

Take another look at the Nebraska football team. Two years ago, a running back was arrested for beating his ex-girlfriend. A few months earlier, two other Nebraska football players were arrested: one for firing two shots

Social Impact of Alcohol in the United States

Drinking is involved in:
  62 percent of all assaults
  54 percent of all murders and attempted murders
  48 percent of all robberies
  44 percent of all burglaries
  42 percent of all rapes[8]

Social Impact of Alcohol in Britain

Drinking is involved in:
  32 percent of all domestic violence
  53 percent of all stranger violence
  45 percent of all acquaintance violence[9]

into a car and another for second degree murder after shooting a man. A task force set up by the university to look into the problem reported that "Alcohol is present in 90 percent of violent incidents reported on campus."[10]

Professional golfer John Daly had his share of problems with alcohol and violence. He said alcohol contributed to his "rude, discourteous, destructive, irresponsible, and insulting" behavior before he quit drinking.[11]

A twenty-year-long study by sociologist Robert Parker recently revealed that the number of homicides is directly related to the number of stores selling alcohol in a community.[12] In addition, a Canadian study showed that 42 percent of all violent crimes in that country are alcohol-related.[13]

The facts are even worse in the United States. A University of Texas study reveals that "90 percent of all sexual assaults involve the use of alcohol."[14] Alcohol and violence are definitely related.

Child Abuse

The United States Department of Health and Human Services oversees The Center for Substance Abuse Prevention. Its former director, Vivian Smith, M.S.W., reported that adults who abuse alcohol are more likely to physically, sexually, or emotionally abuse their children.[15]

According to research from the University of Oklahoma's Center for Child and Family Development, up to 90 percent of parents who abuse their children also abuse drugs and alcohol.[16] Research has shown, however, that treatment is effective and that the incidence of child abuse goes down when parental alcoholism is treated.[17]

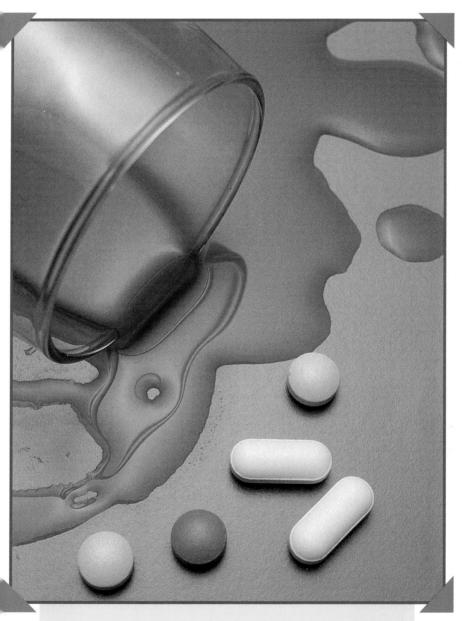

Research indicates that up to 90 percent of parents who abuse their children also abuse drugs and alcohol. However, treatment programs can, and do, reduce the incidence of violence in the home.

Alcohol puts people's inhibitions to sleep. This makes people do things they would never do sober. Drunk driving, violence, and child abuse are just a few of the results.

Fetal Alcohol Syndrome

Another result of alcohol abuse is fetal alcohol syndrome (F.A.S)—a condition in which babies who are born to mothers who drank heavily while pregnant are born abnormally small. These babies may also have severe birth defects. Alcohol that a pregnant woman drinks also goes to the fetus (through the umbilical cord).

Fetal alcohol syndrome is a condition in which babies born to mothers who drank heavily during pregnancy are born abnormally small, often with severe birth defects.

Symptoms of Fetal Alcohol Syndrome

- Behavioral problems
- Droopy eyelids
- Heart defects
- Hyperactivity
- Inability to understand cause and effect
- Irritability
- Learning disabilities
- Low birth weight babies
- Low nasal bridge
- Mental retardation

- Nervousness
- No upper lip groove
- Poor physical abilities
- Seizures
- Short attention span
- Short nose
- Small head
- Small jaw
- Speech problems
- Thin, flat upper lip[18]

Children born with F.A.S can face a lifetime of pain. They must try to survive in a world that does not generally make many allowances for their disabilities.

Lisa's mother could tell you all about the symptoms of F.A.S. Lisa is an F.A.S child. Her mother was drinking during the first two months of her pregnancy. Lisa's mother did not know she was pregnant. She said, "I'm satisfied with Lisa's health, but I wish she didn't have to wear the pacemaker. . . ."[19]

F.A.S is now the leading cause of mental retardation in the United States. It affects more children than Down syndrome.[20]

It is also the leading preventable cause of mental retardation, brought on entirely by drinking during pregnancy.

Binge Drinking

Binge drinking (consuming five or more drinks in one sitting) has become a huge problem among high school and college students.

Diane and John Cole's daughter Valerie, a college freshman, was a binge drinker. Valerie and her best friend, Aleesha, had spent one Saturday evening going from party to party. They had made the rounds of fraternity houses and keg parties. They had been drinking whiskey and washing it down with beer. Sunday morning Aleesha awoke to find Valerie face down on the floor. When she rolled her over, Valerie was cold and purple— she had died from complications of binge drinking.[21]

Alcohol poisoning has claimed the lives of many young people who drank heavily over a short period of time. Although shots of alcohol may seem like harmless fun in a social setting, the results can be deadly.

Binge Drinking in the United States

20 percent of eighteen-year-olds binge drink occasionally.[22]

86 percent of college fraternity members binge drink.[23]

Alcohol poisoning has killed many students. Scott Krueger graduated near the top of his high school class and was accepted at Massachusetts Institute of Technology (MIT), one of the best schools in the country. Friends called 911 when he was not breathing well. He had passed out after drinking sixteen shots of whiskey. Emergency medical personnel found him out cold. He never regained consciousness. Two days later, his parents had his life support systems disconnected.[24]

In May 1997, five students burned to death when a fire swept though their fraternity house in North Carolina. Four of them "may have been too drunk to escape." The fifth may have died trying to save them.[25]

Boating accidents, drownings, fatal falls, suicides, freezing deaths, pedestrian fatalities, divorces, aircraft accidents, and school dropouts are just some of the problems associated with alcohol abuse.

three

I Was a Teenage Alcoholic

The author's interview of Veronica (not her real name) from October 1997 tells of Veronica's problems with alcohol.[1]

"When did you first begin drinking?"

"You'll probably think I'm crazy, but I honestly don't remember! You see, I grew up in a home where my father was alcoholic. At least I guess he was—he was drunk all the time. And my mother used to party with him, not because she was an alcoholic, but to take care of him. And maybe to keep track of him. He'd get pretty wild when he drank."

"What did he do?"

"Well, he'd run off. Sometimes he'd be gone for days. Some of my earliest memories were about my father being drunk. One day, I saw him staggering around the yard. I remember thinking that he was pathetic-looking."

(Seeing that she had tears in her eyes.) "Looks as though that's still painful for you."

"Well, I was the oldest. I was 'daddy's girl.' I guess after I saw him stumbling around like that, something just changed inside of me. I think I started seeing him differently. It was never the same between us after that."

"Let's get back to your drinking for a while."

"OK. I know I was drinking with friends by the time I was twelve. Mostly beer. I remember that I thought it tasted bad. I wondered how my dad could enjoy something that tasted like that. Every time I would drink, I'd need to go to the bathroom.

When I was sixteen, I started going to parties with my friends and drinking Boone's Farm™ Strawberry Wine. That's when I really got into it. I'd drink so much that I'd get sick and throw up. But they'd make you feel out of place if you didn't drink, so I'd do as much as they did."

"Did you ever get a sense that you were getting in too deep?"

"A couple of times. Once I was at a bar with some friends, and..."

"You were at a bar? How old were you?"

"Sixteen."

"How did you get into a bar when you were sixteen?"

"It was easy. In Oklahoma, they didn't put your picture on the driver's licenses."

"Tell me more about that."

Parties with friends can often be a breeding ground for reckless drinking. Wanting to fit in is understandable—but it should never require dangerous behavior.

"Yeah. There was no picture, so we'd just borrow someone's license and show it to the guy at the door. Then, we'd go to the bathroom, open the window, and hand it to a friend. Then, she'd use it to get in. We did this all the time. They never caught on. And besides, they were in the business of selling booze. They never checked closely. If it said you were old enough, you were in. That's all there was to it. Yeah. I got in a fight with my best friend over some guy. She threw beer all over me, and I felt I had to stand up for my rights. It was a pretty bad scene."

"Were there other times?"
"Yeah. Once I got into a situation with some older guys that I regretted later."

"What happened?"
"Well, there were older guys who hung around the school—guys that had already graduated. Some of them were even in college. I shouldn't have gone with them."

"Why not?"
"I was too young to deal with them. I just shouldn't have gone. I never would have done those things if it wasn't for my dad's drinking. It made me feel that getting drunk and acting crazy was normal. Of course, when you're drunk you don't care, so it's twice as bad—not only do you think it's normal, you're drunk and don't care either. But later on you do care, and you feel embarrassed and ashamed. The terrible thing is that feeling like that makes you want to drink more so you don't have to think about it anymore. It's a real trap. Of course, when you're drunk you just do more dumb things."

"Sounds like you've got it pretty well figured out."

"It took a long time. And I had a lot of hard lessons to learn before I got here. One of the problems I had was that I was attracted to guys who were alcoholic. I think that was because my father was one."

"Tell me more about that."

"I started going with one guy when I was thirteen. He was an alcoholic and smoked pot. I smoked with him. He was very controlling and jealous of everyone. If I even spoke to another guy, he thought I wanted to sleep with him. But it wasn't just sexual. He was jealous of my family and girlfriends, too. Actually, I didn't have any girlfriends. He saw to that. Anyway, I started feeling as if he had robbed me of my childhood, so we broke up in my junior year."

"What did you do then?"

"Went crazy. I did the bar scene and stuff. I was wild. I did this for a year, then we got back together. Sounds insane, doesn't it? Well, hang on cause it gets worse. I married him when I was eighteen. We got an apartment, and he got a job in construction. During this time, his drinking really escalated. And he got violent."

"How violent?"

"Well, he tried to strangle me once. That was about a month after we got married. He'd get mad and punch holes in the walls. I used to tape over them with duct tape so my family wouldn't notice them. He threw a full can of beer across the room at me once. It hit me on the hip so hard that my whole side and leg turned black and blue. My foot was so swelled up that I couldn't put my shoe on. Later that day he broke a picture, and when it shattered, some of the glass got in my eye. I had to drive myself to the hospital like that."

"Why did you stay with him?"
"I felt secure with him. It's like I knew what to expect. I got to be an expert at makeup. I could cover up almost any bruise. I should have been a makeup artist. And, you know, when I got home from the hospital, I couldn't find him. Later on, when I talked to him, he didn't even remember doing it."

"What caused you to divorce him?"
"It was when he came after me with the shotgun. He was chasing me though the house, and I ran into the front

Alcoholism is a disease that affects every family member who comes in contact with a drinker.

yard just in time to see my brother go by in his pickup. I remember praying, 'Please God, don't let him see me!' I was afraid he'd come back to help and get killed, too. Later, when I thought about it I realized that I had accepted the fact that he would kill me someday. So, I called my aunts to come and get me."

"So, you were single again?"

"Yeah. But not for long. I married six months later. I hate to tell you this, but he was another alcoholic. In fact, I met him in a bar. He was eleven years older than me, and he owned his own company. We had a child the year after we married. He was into big parties and power trips. He use to give me money, then disappear for a week or two. When I'd ask where he'd been, he'd say, 'I give you money. I don't have to tell you where I go! My job is to earn the money, yours is to take care of the kid.' Finally, I divorced him."

"You don't look old enough to have gone through so much. Do you mind if I ask you how old you are?"

"Twenty-eight. And I've been sober for two years. I just got tired of being sick and tired, so I quit. I started going to Alcoholics Anonymous and working on my issues. It hasn't been easy, but it's sure been worth it."

Veronica is one of the lucky ones. Despite all she's been through, she has survived. She has gone on with her life.

four

Alcohol's Effects on the Body

Not everyone who drinks is destined to become an alcoholic. Some people manage to drink in moderation all their adult lives without suffering severe consequences. In fact, some studies have shown that small amounts of alcohol—a single glass of wine three times a week—can be good for an adult.

On the other hand, using larger amounts of alcohol is always harmful. Used in this way, alcohol damages your body, brain, personality, and relationships.

Physical Problems

Alcohol is a poison.[1] It can damage all of the body's organ systems. That is because it changes the body's basic building blocks—the cells. It does

Small amounts of alcohol—a single glass of wine three times a week—can be beneficial for adults. However, alcohol is a poison that can damage all of the body's systems if it is abused.

this in two ways. It erodes (eats away) tissue, and it sedates (puts to sleep) the cells.[2]

This damage starts with the digestive system. Alcohol inflames every body part it touches. That is why alcohol burns the throat. The esophagus (the tube that goes from your mouth to your stomach) is one of the most seriously damaged areas. If alcohol repeatedly touches the esophagus, it will erode the esophagus lining. This makes it thin and easily damaged. Many alcoholics die from bleeding of the esophageal lining. Alcohol also eats away at the lining of the stomach and intestines. This can cause ulcers, raw or inflamed areas that heal slowly. Ulcers can get so bad that a hole in the stomach may develop. This, too, is often fatal. Alcohol may also cause the stomach to spasm. When this happens, vomiting will result. This can further damage the esophagus. The liver, which has the job of breaking down alcohol, is also damaged. Alcohol burns the liver, causing scars to form. If too much scarring forms (a condition called cirrhosis), the liver will die—and so will its owner.

Another system damaged by too much alcohol use is

Stages of Alcoholism

Early Stage:
- Drinker develops tolerance.
- Drinker has first blackout.
- Drinker sneaks drinks.
- Drinker gulps drinks.
- Drinker has constant thoughts about alcohol.
- Drinker experiences loss of control.

Middle Stage:
- Drinker develops severe guilt.
- Drinker loses friends.
- Drinker experiences chronic anger.
- Drinker has school or work problems.
- Drinker hides alcohol.
- Drinker experiences longer binges.

Late Stage:
- Drinker experiences a decrease in tolerance.
- Drinker is unable to think clearly.
- Drinker's hands shake.
- Drinker drinks to avoid withdrawal.
- Drinker loses hope.
- Drinker may die.[3]

the circulatory system—the heart, arteries, and veins. Alcohol can inflame the heart muscle. When this happens, a condition called myocarditis can result. Alcohol also raises the blood pressure, causing circulatory problems and strokes.

Withdrawal from alcohol can make people going through it feel horrible. The symptoms are profuse sweating, rapid heartbeat, elevated blood pressure, rapid and shallow breathing, and excessive anxiety.

In addition to these symptoms, some people get delirium tremens (the DT's). A person with the DT's will shake excessively and hallucinate (see things that aren't there—like snakes or bugs crawling on them). During this time, their blood pressure will reach extremely dangerous levels. About half of those who get the DT's will die eventually if they don't get medical attention.[4]

Types of Alcoholism

There seem to be three types of alcoholics. The first are those people who are born alcoholic. They inherit a gene that makes them vulnerable to become addicted to alcohol. Dr. Henry Begleiter is a researcher at the State University of New York at Brooklyn. He has discovered new facts about these "born alcoholics." His research has shown that the gene that makes someone vulnerable to alcoholism can be passed from either mother or father to son or daughter. These alcoholics start to drink later than others, perhaps in their late teens or early twenties. They might even wait until their forties or fifties before they start drinking. For them, alcoholism takes many years to develop. Dr. Begleiter has also shown that sometimes the gene passes only from father to son. These alcoholics tend to start drinking very early—sometimes before the age of twelve. They usually become full-blown alcoholics in a matter of a few months to a year. They can tolerate large amounts of alcohol, often drinking their peers "under the table." They are often violent when they drink, and as a result may get into trouble with the authorities.[5]

Stress-Induced Drinkers

The second type of alcoholics are stress-induced drinkers. These alcoholics drink when under stress. However, they drink so much that they temporarily damage their brain chemistry to such an extent that they lose their ability to feel good without drinking. This can turn them into alcoholics, because their brain chemistry has become abnormal.[6]

Research indicates that there seem to be several types of alcoholics. Regardless of the type of drinker, alcoholism is a serious disease that left untreated can be deadly.

Permanent Brain Damage

The third type of alcoholics are much like the second type. The main difference is that the damage to their brain is permanent. This means that their alcoholism is much more long-term and may even become permanent.[7]

Mental Problems

An MRI (a very sophisticated test resembling an X ray) reveals that alcohol slowly causes the destruction of brain cells. This makes the brain increasingly incapable of thinking clearly. Dr. John Wallace (Medical Director of Edgehill Newport Clinic) has done research that reveals the damage can be permanent.[8] This means that every time a person drinks, thousands of brain cells are destroyed. Drinkers' brains become less efficient with every drink.

There is a commonly accepted myth that alcohol stimulates the brain, making people happier and more competent. This is not the case. Once alcohol enters the brain, it begins deadening it. The process starts at the front of the brain and slowly moves to the rear. Because the part of the brain that controls reason, judgment, and inhibition is in the front, they are the first qualities to be put to sleep. This makes people feel momentarily uninhibited.[9] The proof that alcohol is a poison that slowly paralyzes the brain becomes apparent with alcohol's effect on the rest of the brain. When alcohol hits the midbrain, it disrupts the part of the brain that controls speech, memory, coordination, and depth perception (ability to correctly perceive how far away things are).[10] This is why people who are drunk stagger, slur their

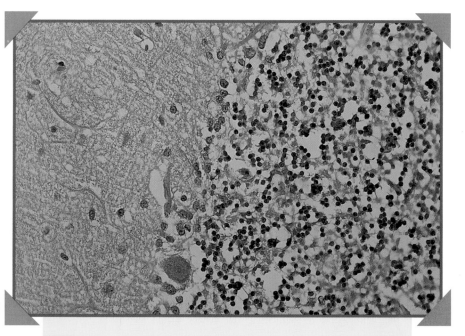

This is what healthy brain tissue looks like. Alcohol abuse can result in the destruction of brain tissue.

words, have difficulty remembering, bump into things, and have traffic accidents.

When alcohol reaches the back part of the brain, the results can be fatal. This is the part of the brain that controls heartbeat and breathing. When people drink enough to put this part of the brain to sleep, they "pass out" (go into an alcohol-induced coma). Some never wake up. They simply die. (For examples of this, read the section titled "Binge Drinking" in Chapter 2.)

Alcoholics may also begin to have "blackouts" (times when they can't recall what they did or said). In fact, this is often one of the first recognizable symptoms of alcoholism. It may start as soon as six months after the onset of drinking behavior. This is difficult for new drinkers to understand, so most of them "confabulate," filling in the blanks with a series of made-up events.[11] Over time, they become very convinced of these self-lies. This can be extremely confusing to others who were there and know what actually happened.

Chronic drinkers may eventually develop "wet brain." This phrase refers to a permanently disabled brain that simply gets everything wrong. These people slowly lose control of bodily functions to the point that they cannot control their bowel or bladder. They will then soil their clothes.

After a time, the brain may begin to atrophy or shrink. Once this process begins, death will eventually result. But it will be a very slow and painful death. Eventually, the victim's brain will not be able to send signals to the heart, telling it to beat, or to the lungs, telling them to breathe.[12]

Personality Problems

Dr. Robert Ackerman is a professor of sociology at Indiana State University. He has dedicated his life to the study of alcoholism. He claims that alcoholics develop certain personality problems. They may deny that a problem exists, but blame others for the problem. They may also spend money for important needs on alcohol, or become unpredictable. They may become verbally or physically abusive, and feel hopeless and suicidal.[13]

Dr. George Vaillant of the Dartmouth Medical School says that alcoholism is a disease that makes people overly angry at those they love most. This certainly would explain the level of domestic violence associated with alcohol use.[14]

All of these factors make alcohol abusers very difficult

Alcoholic's Anonymous's Twelve Questions

1. Have you ever decided to stop drinking for a week or so, but only lasted for a couple of days?

2. Do you wish people would mind their own business about your drinking—stop telling you what to do?

3. Have you ever switched from one kind of drink to another in the hope that this would keep you from getting drunk?

4. Have you ever had to have an "eye-opener" drink upon awakening (or to stop shaking) during the last year?

5. Do you envy people who can drink without getting into trouble?

6. Have you had problems connected with drinking during the past two years?

7. Has your drinking caused trouble at home?

8. Do you ever get "extra" drinks at a party because you did not get enough?

9. Do you tell yourself that you can stop drinking anytime you want to, even though you keep getting drunk when you don't mean to?

10. Have you missed days of work or school because of drinking?

11. Do you have blackouts?

12. Have you ever felt that your life would be better if you did not drink?

Did you answer "yes" four times or more? If so, you're probably in trouble with alcohol.[15]

to live with and causes numerous problems for their families.

Family Problems

Anyone who lives in a family in which one or more of the members is alcoholic is affected by the alcoholic's drinking. And they are affected in very specific ways. They are "co-alcoholics" or "codependents."

According to alcohol counselor Robert Subby, codependents have difficulty with intimacy. They can't identify and express feelings. They also have difficulty making decisions, feel powerless, and obsessively seek approval. All of these problems are a result of low self-esteem. They are also rigid and perfectionists, which makes it difficult for them to adjust to change. They avoid conflict and feel responsible for other people's behavior.[16]

According to Dr. Claudia Black, author of *It Will Never Happen to Me*, children in codependent families are especially deeply affected. There is a great deal of the pain associated with living in a family with an alcoholic member. As a coping mechanism for this pain, these children develop certain dysfunctional roles. Dr. Black has referred to these roles as The Responsible One, The Adjuster, and The Placator. She describes the responsible one as the person who takes over the alcoholic's job in the family. The responsible one seeks to protect both the alcoholic and the family from the consequences of alcoholism. The placator does his or her best to minimize the conflicts in alcoholic families. This protects everyone from the outbursts of anger. The adjuster is the person who adapts quickly to the radical changes in the alcoholic family. One moment the alcoholic is being

A strong, supportive family with loving relationships is essential to learning how to develop healthy relationships with others.

thrown out of the family, the next he or she is being begged to stay. In adjusting to these extremes, this person loses all sense of self, but, like the placator, lowers the conflict in the family.[17]

Janet Woititz, author of *Children of Alcoholics*, has shown that these problems can last a lifetime. Long after the child has married and moved away, he or she will probably have difficulty with intimacy and low self-esteem.[18] There is even evidence that the stress of being in the same family with an alcohol abuser can cause numerous physical illnesses.[19]

five

Fighting
Back

There are many ways to fight alcohol abuse and addiction. The trick is getting the drinker to want to quit. Once a drinker reaches this point, research has shown that youth involvement is one of the most effective ways of fighting alcohol abuse.[1]

D.A.R.E.

Some programs may be available through your local police department. The D.A.R.E. (Drug Abuse Resistance Education) program is one example. The D.A.R.E. program usually starts in the fifth grade. Police officers come into the school to deliver speeches about drug use, refusal skills, and self-esteem. Students can become involved by functioning as leaders of support groups for students who participate.[2]

Project Northland

Project Northland is a Minnesota prevention project that has been highly effective. In fact, this project has been so successful in changing the drinking behavior of young people that it may serve as a model for projects in other states. This project is a combination of action-oriented youth training and leadership with parental and community participation. The key to this program is getting everyone to work together. Those who are interested in starting a similar program in their school should write the Robert Wood Johnson Foundation (P.O. Box 3216, Princeton, N.J. 08543-2316), <http://www.rwjf.org>.[3]

Responsible Alcohol and Tobacco Sales Training (RATS)

One of the newer prevention programs is Responsible Alcohol and Tobacco Sales Training (RATS). This program trains local businesses and their employees how to respond to youths who try to purchase alcohol and tobacco products. RATS is always in need of young people to act as part of their training team. Those who become RATS trainers go into stores and try to buy beer or cigarettes. The clerk will be expecting the trainee. The trainee's job is to help the clerk practice his or her refusal skills. Those interested can call or write the Department of Substance Abuse Prevention in their state capital for more information and to learn whether the program is operating in that state.[4]

La Esperanza del Valle

A special program for communities with a large Hispanic population is La Esperanza del Valle. Programs such as this are extremely important now that Hispanics are the largest ethnic minority group in the United States. This program was developed by the Yakima Coalition of Hispanics for a Drug Free Society. A series of meetings revealed that alcohol misuse was the single biggest problem for Hispanics living in Yakima Valley, Washington. After much discussion, it was decided that the best approach to dealing with the problem was to involve Hispanic youths themselves in the solution. The young people decided to write plays addressing the issues of alcohol and drug use. The plays were then shown on television, played on the radio, and printed in newspapers. The outcome was exceptional. Alcohol abuse reached an all-time low in the valley.[5]

Youths With a Vision for St. Louis

Another prevention project that uses young people to help address the issues of alcohol abuse is the Youth With a Vision for St. Louis campaign. The theme of this campaign is "It's our life, why not. . ." The focus is on young people answering this question for themselves and their peers. They do this on posters, billboard advertising, and radio and television commercials. These media efforts are also directed at parents and other adults, asking them to help create a safe environment for youths to grow up in.[6]

Zuni Communication Project

The Zuni Communication Project started with the formation of groups of New Mexico tribes' elders and youths. After these groups were formed, a three-stage needs assessment was done. This three-stage process

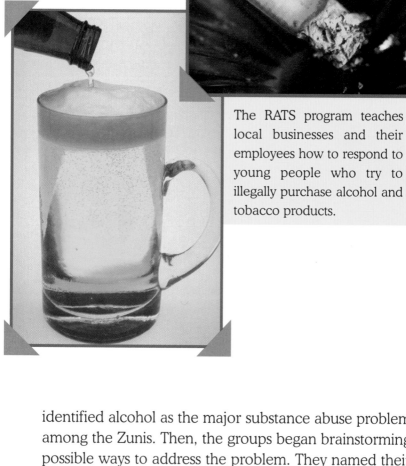

The RATS program teaches local businesses and their employees how to respond to young people who try to illegally purchase alcohol and tobacco products.

identified alcohol as the major substance abuse problem among the Zunis. Then, the groups began brainstorming possible ways to address the problem. They named their program "Raise the Roof for Zuni Teenagers." Soon the group adopted a strategy of designing a logo and slogans for posters, hats, and T-shirts. They also created two videos, "The Creation Story" and "The Prophecy." Because elders are so important in their culture, the videos feature elders telling important tribal stories in the Zuni language and in English.[7]

Young people have many alternatives to alcohol for entertainment. Relationships with friends should be based on a wide variety of healthy, safe, shared activities.

The Michigan Model

While many people just talk about the alcohol and drug problem, the more effective ones get involved in finding a solution even if that means fighting the establishment. That's exactly what Barbara Fils of Northville, Michigan, did. School officials were reluctant to continue a prevention project. So she organized a group of community leaders to look into the issue. They met and went over the program piece by piece. When they were convinced that it was sound, they met with school officials and voiced their opinions. The result has become known as The Michigan Model. It has been in existence for more than eight years, and it is still working.[8]

six

What Can Be Done

The best thing that young people can do to avoid becoming alcoholic is to find ways to take care of themselves. This is not always easy, but it is the best shot at success. Here are some options.

Leading a Healthy Lifestyle

Young people often do not have a healthy lifestyle. It's not just that some drink. They may not get enough exercise or eat right. And many are simply stressed out. Maybe some are too busy. Americans and Canadians live in two of the wealthiest countries in the world. Still our citizens do not always do those things that they know would make them healthier people.

If they were to develop a healthy lifestyle, they would be happier and healthier and would have less time to become involved with alcohol abuse.

Resisting Peer Pressure

Unfortunately, just leading a healthy lifestyle may not be enough for some people. This is especially true for people whose peers (people their own age) may be drinkers. They may push other young people to drink.[1] It can be hard for young people to say no to people they care about—or to people whose opinions they are worried about.

On the other hand, why should a person care about someone who would try to force them to do something they know is not good for them?

Every young person who is tempted to start drinking because of peer pressure should ask himself or herself what will be gained by yielding to that pressure.

Leading a healthy, drug-free lifestyle means exercising regularly and eating right.

Find a Self-Help Group

Those who cannot stop drinking may need the support and encouragement found in a self-help group. The group with the longest history and best track record is Alcoholics Anonymous (AA).[2] Each AA group is filled with people who have had difficulty leaving alcohol alone. They've been helping people for years. Group locations can be found in the white pages of the telephone book. AA's World Service office can also help. Their number is listed in the back of this book under "Helpful Numbers."

Many churches and synagogues have self-help groups. Some may have an Overcomer's Outreach group. A call to a priest, pastor, or rabbi may be helpful in locating one.

Get Into Treatment

Some people are so addicted to alcohol that they need more than a self-help group to quit drinking. They need professional help. They may attend a self-help group but keep right on drinking. This is an indication that they need more help than the group can provide. This is also true if they find that after getting sober, they start drinking again. In either of these cases, they need to find an alcoholism counselor.

The yellow pages is a good place to begin that search. They should look under "Alcohol Counselors," "Drug Counselors," or "Alcohol Treatment Centers." It's best to look for someone who has letters like these after their names:

◆ "CADC" (Certified Alcohol and Drug Counselor)

- "NCADC" (National Certified Alcohol and Drug Counselor)

- "MAC" (Master Addiction Counselor)

- "ICADC" (International Certified Alcohol and Drug Counselor)

These designations mean that these counselors have met state, national, or international training requirements.[3] It's one way of ensuring that the counselor you choose will be helpful.

Additional hotlines are listed in the back of this book.

questions
for discussion

1. What would you say to a friend who wanted to start drinking?

2. Some people think that their drinking only hurts themselves. What do you think?

3. Why do some people want to fight when they drink?

4. Your best friend says that you can't become alcoholic drinking beer. Do you agree or disagree?

5. Two of your friends are talking about having a drinking contest. Do you think this is wise?

6. An older teen says that you have to drink a long time to become an alcoholic. What do you think?

7. You're at a party when a friend offers you a beer. How would you handle it?

8. Your sister says that it doesn't hurt to drive if you've only had a couple of wine coolers. What do you think?

9. Do alcohol advertisements work? Do teens who see television ads for beer actually go out and drink? If so, what should be done about alcohol advertising?

10. Is there any reason to believe that some people are born with a tendency to become alcoholic?

11. Some people believe that alcohol is not as dangerous to teenagers as are drugs. What do you think?

12. If you knew that a pregnant friend was drinking, what advice would you give her?

13. Is there anything wrong with making a decision to never drink alcohol?

14. Despite all the evidence of alcohol's harmful effects, people continue to use it. Why do you think this is true?

15. There are laws against selling alcohol to underage people. Even so, teenage drinking has reached epidemic proportions. What do you think can be done about it?

chapter notes

Chapter 1. A Popular Poison

1. Author interview with "Jon," August 22, 1997.

2. L. D. Johnson et. al., *Monitoring the Future Study* (Rockville, Md.: The National Institute on Drug Abuse, 1994).

3. Kenneth Gerew, ed., *Lets All Fight Drug Abuse* (Dallas: L.A.W. Publications, 1992), p. 2.

4. Johnson, et al.

5. Ibid.

Chapter 2. The Social Impact of Alcohol

1. Casey O'Connor, "The Moment of Truth," *The Express Line*, September 10–11, 1997, p. 2.

2. Zachary Boose, *Drinking & Driving* (Norman, Okla.: Area Prevention Resource Center, 1995), p. 6.

3. Christopher Dickey and Mark Hosenball, "A Needless Tragedy," *Newsweek*, September 22, 1997, pp. 1–3.

4. Christopher Dickey and Sharon Begley, "A Deadly Puzzle," *Newsweek*, October 15, 1997, pp. 2–4.

5. Roger Pugh, "Matlis' Killer Was Drunk," *Piedmont-Surry Hills Gazette*, January 3, 1993, p. 1.

6. "John Verdal Suspended by Osborne," *College Football Notes*, <http://www.onwis.com/sports/coll/cfb/1218.html>, p. 1.

7. Charles Chandler, "Whitley Out for Drunk Driving," *The Charlotte Observer*, October 31, 1996, p. 3.

8. *Correlation to Crime & Violence*, Center for Substance Abuse Prevention, 1995, pp. 1–2.

9. *Drink Fuels Increase in Violent Crime*, Home Office Statistical Bulletin of the 1996 British Crime Survey for England and Wales, September 1996, pp. 1–2.

10. The University of Austin Home Page, <http://www.utexas.adi.admin/utpd/authority.html>, April 16, 1996, p. 1.

11. "Unexplained Mysteries of Professional Sports," *The Sporting News*, July 25, 1997, p. 1.

12. Chris Bigsby, Erin Ratcliff, and Letitia Rexrode, "The Myths and Facts of Alcohol," Radford's Home Page Radford University, <http://renet.edu/~cmoore>, April 15, 1996, p. 1.

13. Marta Sinha, "Daiquiris and Drive-bys," *The MoJo Wire Service*, Foundation for National Progress, October 11, 1997, p. 2.

14. "The University of Texas at Austin Police Department Home Page," <http://www.utexas.adi.admin/utpd/authority.html>, April 16, 1996, p. 2.

15. Vivian Smith, "From the Director of CSAP," *Child Abuse* (Rockville, Md.: November 1992), p. 1.

16. *Substance Abuse Is Not a Black and White Issue: It's Black and Blue* (Rockville, Md.: Center for Child and Family Development, 1994), p. 3.

17. *Correlates of Child Abuse* (Rockville, Md.: National Institute on Alcohol and Drug Abuse, 1997), p. 23.

18. *Fetal Alcohol Syndrome* (Rockville, Md.: National Clearinghouse for Alcohol and Drug Information), pp. 1–4.

19. "Lisa's mother," *Preventing FAS*, videocassette (Province of British Columbia: LENA Productions, 1991).

20. *Fetal Alcohol Syndrome*, p. 3.

21. *Message from Secretary of Health and Human Services, Donna E. Shalala* (Rockville, Md.: National Institute on Alcohol and Alcoholism, No. 29 PH, July 1995), pp. 1–6.

22. "Alcoholic Newscaster Sobers Up," *The Oprah Scoop*, October 22, 1997, pp. 1–2.

23. "Beer, Part 2," *Consumer Reports*, June 1996, p. 4.

24. "Alcoholic Newscaster Sobers Up," pp. 1–2.

25. Claudia Kalb, "Society Colleges: Drinking and Dying," *Newsweek*, October 13, 1997, p. 1.

Chapter 3. I Was a Teenage Alcoholic

1. Author interview with "Veronica," October 26, 1997.

Chapter 4. Alcohol's Effects on the Body

1. Bill Blakemore, *ABC News Close Up: "Alcohol & Cocaine,"* videocassette, Dir. Richard Gerdau (American Broadcasting Company, 1987).

2. Max Schneider, *Medical Aspects of Alcoholism*, videocassette, Dir. Timothy Armstrong (FMS Productions, 1991).

3. "A Chart of Alcohol Addiction," Oklahoma City: A Chance to Change Foundation., p. 1.

4. Schneider.

5. Henri Begleiter, *ABC News Close Up: "Alcohol & Cocaine,"* videocassette, Dir. Richard Gerdau (American Broadcasting Company, 1987).

6. "Alcoholism," *The World Book Multimedia Encyclopedia*, (Chicago: World Book, 1996).

7. Ibid.

8. John Wallace, M.D., *ABC News Close Up: "Alcohol & Cocaine,"* videocassette, Dir. Richard Gerdau (American Broadcasting Company, 1987.)

9. Davis Ohlms, *The Disease Concept of Alcoholism, Part I*, videocassette, Dir. Sherry Jarrett (Gary Whitaker Company, 1982).

10. Ibid.

11. Davis Ohlms, *The Disease Concept of Alcoholism, Part II*, videocassette, Dir. Sherry Jarrett (Gary Whitaker Company, 1982).

12. Ibid.

13. David Ackerman, "Alcoholism and the Family," *Growing in the Shadow: Children of Alcoholics* (Pompano Beach, Fla.: Health Communications, 1985), p. 11.

14. George Vaillant, *ABC News Close Up: "Alcohol & Cocaine,"* videocassette, Dir. Richard Gerdau (American Broadcasting Company, 1987).

15. "Is AA For You," Alcoholics Anonymous World Services, 1998, <http://www.Alcoholics-Anonymous.org/ep3dol.html>.

16. Robert Subby, *Lost in the Shuffle: The Co-dependent Reality* (Deerfield Beach, Fla.: Health Communications, 1987), pp. 16–17.

17. Claudia Black, "Children of Alcoholics," *Growing in the Shadow: Children of Alcoholics*, Robert Ackerman, ed. (Pompano Beach, Fla.: Health Communications), pp. 106–107.

18. Janet Woiltitz, *Adult Children of Alcoholics* (Pompano Beach, Fla.: Health Communications, 1983), p. 23.

19. Max Schneider, *Medical Aspects of Codependency*, videocassette, Dir. Kathryn Connell (FMS Productions, 1991).

Chapter 5. Fighting Back

1. "Getting It Together: Promoting Drug-Free Communities," *A Resource Guide for Developing Effective Youth Coalitions* (Rockville, Md.: U.S. Department of Health and Human Services, Public Health Service, 1991), PHD 579.

2. William Hansen and Ralph McNeal, "How D.A.R.E. Works," *Health Education & Behavior*, vol. 24, no. 2, April 1997, pp. 165–176.

3. Henry Wechsler and Elissa Weirzman, "Community Solutions to Community Problems—Preventing Adolescent Alcohol Use," *Journal of Public Health*, vol. 86, no. 7, July 1996, pp. 923–925.

4. "Responsible Alcohol and Tobacco Sales Training," *Health Education Quarterly*, vol. 23, no. 4, November 1996, pp. 416–417.

5. Bernadette LaLonde et. al. "La Esperanza del Valle: Alcohol Prevention for Hispanic Youth and Their Families," *Health Education & Behavior*, vol. 24, no. 5, October 1997, pp. 587–602.

6. "It's Our Life, Why Not...?" *Health Education & Behavior*, vol. 24, no. 5, October 1997, pp. 540–541.

7. "Raise the Roof! The Zuni Communication Project," *Health Education & Behavior*, vol. 24, no. 5, October 1997, pp. 534–535.

8. Ziba Kashef, "Tackling Drug Prevention," *Good Housekeeping*, October 1996, pp. 172, 174.

Chapter 6. What Can Be Done

1. George Berger, *The Pressure to Take Drugs* (New York: Franklin Watts, 1990), p. 27.

2. *Alcoholic Anonymous* (New York: Alcoholics Anonymous World Services, 1996), p. xi.

3. Mimmie Byrne et. al., *Role Delineation Study for Alcohol and Drug Abuse Counselors* (Raleigh, N.C.: National Certification Reciprocity Consortium, 1991), p. 1.

where to write

Al-Anon/Alateen Family Group Headquarters
1600 Corporate Landing Pkwy
Virginia Beach, VA 23454-5617
1-800-344-2666
<http://www.al-anon.alateen.org>

Alcoholics Anonymous (AA) World Services
475 Riverside Drive
New York, NY 10115
1-212-870-3400
<http://www.alcoholics-anonymous.org/>

Center for Substance Abuse Prevention
Rockwall II, 9th Floor
5600 Fishers Lane
Rockville, MD 20857
1-301-443-0365
<http://covesoft.com/csap.html>

Hazelden Foundation Education Materials
P. O. Box 176
Center City, MN 55012
1-800-328-9000
<http://www.hazelden.org/>

Mothers Against Drug Driving (MADD)
511 East John Carpenter Freeway
Suite 700
Irving, TX 75062
1-800-GET-MADD
<http://www.madd.org/>

National Association of Alcohol and Drug Counselors
1911 North Fort Myer Drive
Suite 900
Arlington, VA 22209
1-703-741-7686
<http://www.naadac.org/>

National Association for Children of Alcoholics
11426 Rockville Pike
Suite 100
Rockville, MD 20852
1-301-468-0985
<http://www.health.org/nacoa>

**National Association of Native American
Children of Alcoholics**
1402 3rd Avenue
Suite 1110
Seattle, WA 98101
1-206-467-7686
<http://www.nanacoa.org/>

National Black Child Development Institute
463 Rhode Island Avenue, NW
Washington, DC 20005
1-202-387-1281
<http://www.nbcdi.org/>

National Clearinghouse for Alcohol and Drug Abuse
204 Monroe Street
Rockville, MD 20852
1-301-468-2600
<http://www.health.org/>

National Coalition of Hispanic Health & Human Services Orgs.
1501 16th Street, NW
Washington, DC 20005
1-202-387-5000
<http://www.cossmho.org/>

National Council on Alcoholism and Drug Dependence
12 West 21st Street, 7th Floor
New York, NY 10010
1-800-622-2255
<http://www.ncadd.org/>

National Families in Action
2957 Clairmont Road, Suite 150
Atlanta, GA 30329
1-404-248-9676
<http://www.emory.edu/NFIA/>

Students Against Drunk Driving (SADD)
200 Pleasant Street
Marlboro, MA 01752
1-508-481-3568
<http://www.SADD.org/>

HOTLINES

Alcohol Treatment Referral Hotline
1-800-ALCOHOL
(This service provides a 24 hour help
and referral service.)

Center for Substance Abuse Treatment Hotline
1-800-662-HELP
(They help callers find treatment in their communities.)

National Domestic Violence Hotline
1-800-333-SAFE
(For help with violence in the home.)

Spanish Language Hotline
1-800-66-AYUDA
(This line is staffed by people who speak Spanish.)

Teen Helpline
1-800-400-0900
(They help teens with all kinds of problems, including those associated with alcohol.)

further reading

Berger, Gabriel. *The Pressure to Take Drugs*. New York: Franklin Watts, 1990.

Clayton, Lawrence. *Barbiturates and Other Depressants*. New York: Rosen Publishing, 1997.

———. *Coping With a Drug Abusing Parent*. New York: Rosen Publishing, 1995.

———. *Tranquilizers*. Springfield, N.J.: Enslow Publishers, Inc., 1997.

Kaplan, Linda. *Coping With Peer Pressure*. New York: Rosen Publishing Group, 1993.

Landau, Elaine. *Teenage Drinking*. Hillside, N.J.: Enslow Publishers, 1994.

Minnesota Prevention Resource Center. *Drugs and Family Violence*. Anoka, Minn.: Minnesota Department of Human Services, 1991.

Monroe, Judy. *Alcohol*. Hillside, N.J.: Enslow Publishers, 1994.

Poterfield, Marie. *Coping With an Alcoholic Parent*. New York: Rosen, 1990.

Spence, Wayne. *Alcohol and the Family*. Waco, Tex.: Health EDCO, 1990.

———. *Alcohol and Pregnancy: Keeping Your Baby Sober*. Waco, Tex.: Health EDCO, 1991.

———. *Alcohol and You: A Guide for Teenagers*. Waco, Tex.: Health EDCO, 1994.

———. *Alcoholism: The Medical Consequences*. Waco, Tex.: Health EDCO, 1994.

———. *Children of Alcoholics: Growing Up Amidst Pain*. Waco, Tex.: Health EDCO, 1994.

———. *Drinking and Driving*. Waco, Tex.: Health EDCO, 1993.

Youth and Family Services. *About Alcohol, Child Abuse, and Child Neglect*. Trenton, N.J.: New Jersey Department of Human Services, 1989.

Internet Addresses

Alcohol Dependence (Alcoholism)
<http://beWELL.com/hic/alcoholism/>

National Institute on Alcohol Abuse and Alcoholism
<http://www.niaaa.nih.gov/>

index